Tomorrow's Alphabet

By
George Shannon
Pictures by
Donald Crews

Greenwillow Books, New York

Watercolors were used for the full-color art. The text type is Akzidenz Grotesk.

Tomorrow's Alphabet
Text copyright © 1996
by George W. B. Shannon
Illustrations copyright © 1996
by Donald Crews

First Edition 10

Manufactured in China
by South China Printing
Company Ltd.

www.harperchildrens.com

Library of Congress
Cataloging-in-Publication Data

Shannon, George.
Tomorrow's alphabet / by
George Shannon;
pictures by Donald Crews.
    p.   cm.

"Greenwillow Books."
1. English language—Alphabet—
Juvenile literature.
[1. Alphabet.]   I. Crews,
Donald, ill.   II. Title.
PE1155.S5   1996   [E]—dc20
94-19484   CIP   AC
ISBN 0-688-13504-8 (trade)
ISBN 0-688-13505-6 (lib. bdg.)
ISBN 0-688-16424-2 (pbk.)

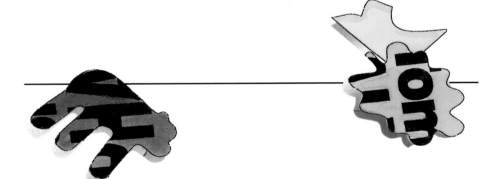

A is for seed–

tomorrow's

APPLE

B is for eggs—

tomorrow's

BIRDS

C is for milk–

tomorrow's

CHEESE

D

**is for
puppy–**

tomorrow's

DOG

E is for campfire—

tomorrow's

EMBERS

F is for wheat–

tomorrow's

FLOUR

G

is for
bulbs–

tomorrow's

GARDEN

H

is for yarn–

tomorrow's

HAT

is for water–

tomorrow's

ICE CUBES

J **is for
pumpkin–**

tomorrow's

JACK-O'-LANTERN

K is for
tomato–

tomorrow's

BEST
KETCHUP
HIMMELS

KETCHUP

L

is for bud–

tomorrow's

LEAF

M

is for caterpillar–

tomorrow's

MOTH

N is for twigs—

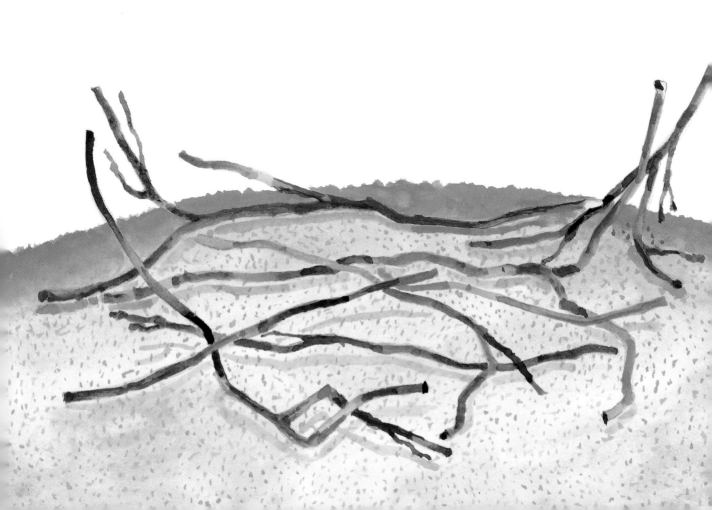

tomorrow's

NEST

O **is for acorn–**

tomorrow's

OAK TREE

P
is for clay–

tomorrow's

POT

Q

is for scraps–

tomorrow's

QUILT

R

is for grapes–

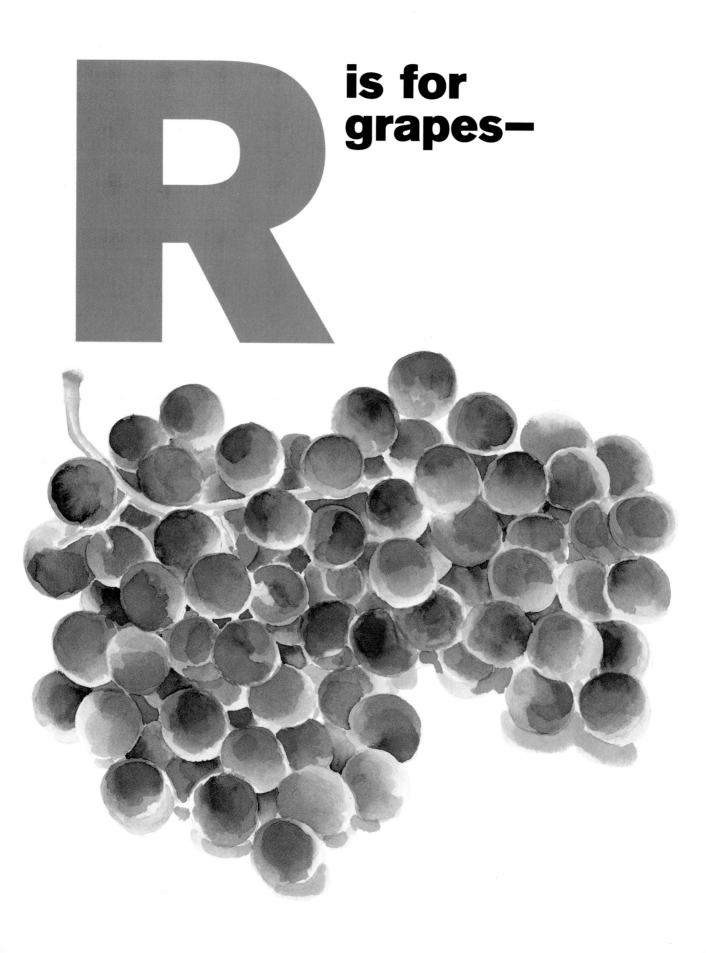

S is for vegetables–

tomorrow's

SOUP

T is for
bread–

tomorrow's

TOAST

U is for stranger–

tomorrow's

US

V is for paper–

tomorrow's

BE MY VALENTINE

VALENTINE

W is for stones—

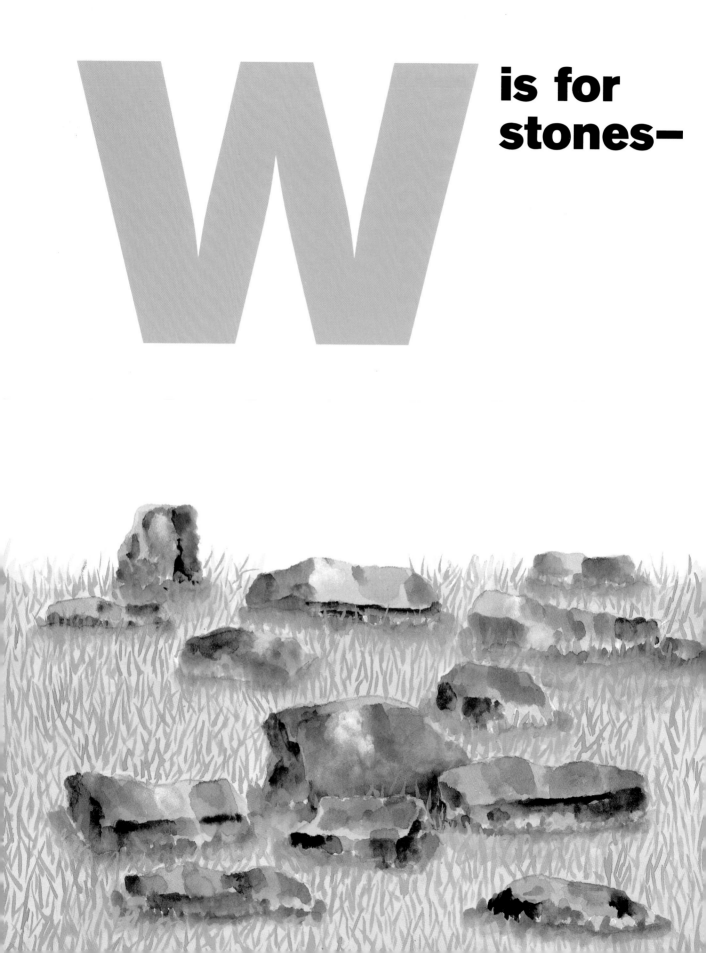

tomorrow's

WALL

X

is for bones—

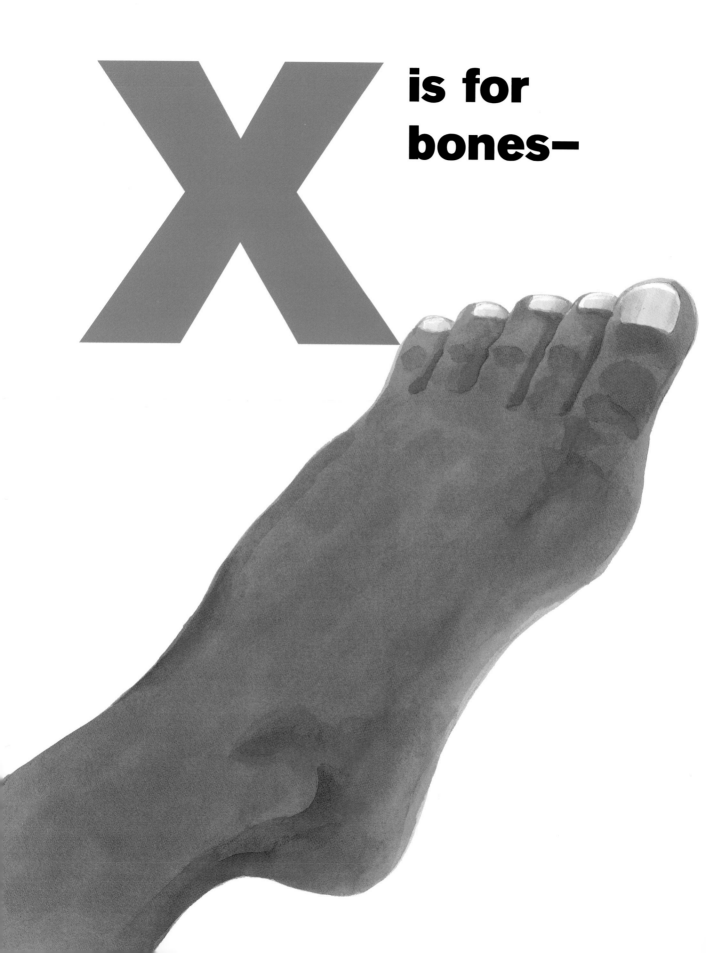

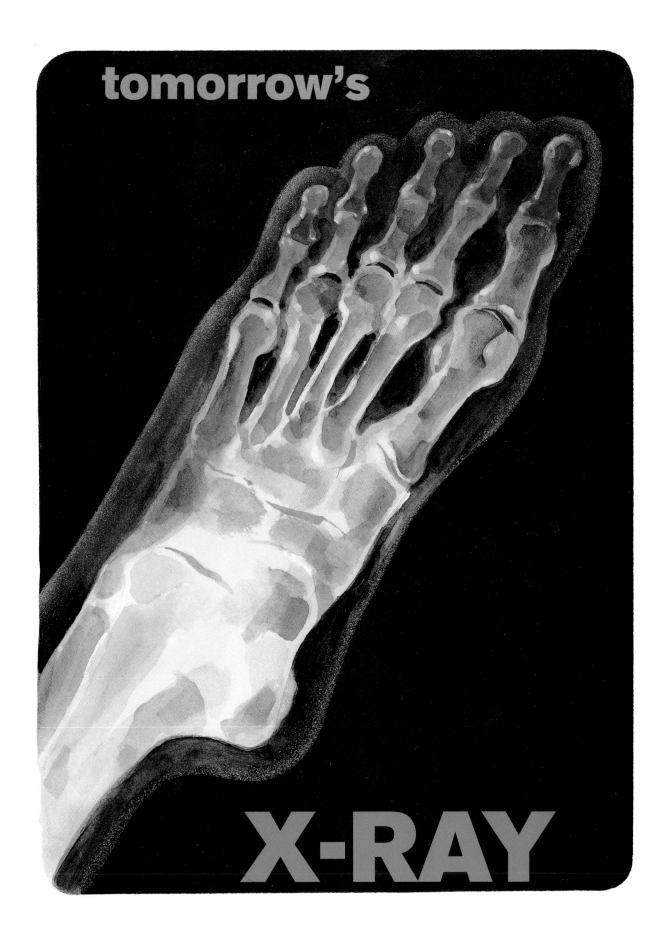

Y is for sheep–

tomorrow's

100% WOOL

YARN

Z is for countdown–

9 8 7 6 5 4 3 2 1

tomorrow's

ZERO